Jem and the Golden Reward

Goldtown Beginnings Series

Jem Strikes Gold
Jem's Frog Fiasco
Jem and the Mystery Thief
Jem Digs Up Trouble
Jem and the Golden Reward
Jem's Wild Winter

Jem and the
Golden Reward

REWARD
$2000

LOST DOG

Susan K. Marlow
Illustrated by Okan Bülbül

KREGEL
PUBLICATIONS

Jem and the Golden Reward
© 2020 by Susan K. Marlow

Published by Kregel Publications, a division of Kregel Inc., 2450 Oak
Industrial Dr. NE, Grand Rapids, MI 49505.

Library of Congress Cataloging-in-Publication Data
Names: Marlow, Susan K., author. | Bülbül, Okan, illustrator.
Title: Jem and the golden reward / Susan K. Marlow ; [Okan Bülbül]
Description: Grand Rapids, MI : Kregel Publications, [2020] | Series:
    Goldtown beginnings ; #5 | Audience: Ages 6–8. |
Identifiers: LCCN 2020019563 (print) | LCCN 2020019564 (ebook) |
Subjects: CYAC: Lost and found possessions—Fiction. | Golden
    retriever—Fiction. | Dogs—Fiction. | Gold mines and mining—
    Fiction. | Family life—California—Fiction. | Christian life—Fiction.
    | California—History—1850–1950—Fiction.
Classification: LCC PZ7.M34528 Jec 2020 (print) |
    LCC PZ7.M34528 (ebook) | DDC [Fic]—dc23
LC record available at https://lccn.loc.gov/2020019563
LC ebook record available at https://lccn.loc.gov/2020019564

ISBN 978-0-8254-4629-0, print
ISBN 978-0-8254-7629-7, epub

Printed in the United States of America
20 21 22 23 24 25 26 27 28 29 / 5 4 3 2 1

Contents

New Words 7

1. September Storm 9
2. First Day of School 17
3. Something to See 24
4. The Reward Poster 31
5. Trouble 36
6. Unwelcome Visitor 43
7. Jem's Not-So-Great Idea 50
8. A Night in the Woods 57
9. Danger! 64
10. Gold Nugget Telegram 72

A Peek into the Past: Rattlesnake Bites . . . 79

New Words

Aye (*I*)—a Scottish word that means "yes"
Bootjack—a gold camp near Goldtown
delighted—pleased, happy
echoed—a sound that repeats over and over
  after the first sound is made
laddie—a boy
misery—a deep sadness
och (*auck*)—a Scottish word that shows
  surprise
retriever—a breed of dog that brings ducks
  and other birds back to a hunter
'rithmetic—a short way of saying
  arithmetic; math
Scotland—a small country in Europe; part
  of the island of Great Britain

telegram—a message sent over telegraph wires

venom—poison from a rattlesnake or other animal

CHAPTER 1

September Storm

"Jeremiah!"

Jem sucked in his breath. Mama meant business when she used his full first name.

"Jeremiah Isaiah Coulter!"

Roasted rattlesnakes!

Did Mama have to shout Jem's whole, entire name so it was heard by every miner along Cripple Creek?

He looked around.

Half a dozen miners were lined up on their gold claims.

They didn't pay any attention to Mama's shouts. They were too busy panning for gold.

A sudden rainstorm had filled the creek overnight. Everybody was surprised.

Especially Jem. It never rained in September.

Well, almost never.

Last night's thunderstorm had dumped buckets of rain. The muddy trickle had turned into a rushing creek.

Quick as a wink, Jem had grabbed his gold pan this morning and headed for the creek. He didn't even eat breakfast.

A gold miner never knew how long the water would flow this time of year.

"Jeremiah Isai—"

"Coming, Mama!" Jem hollered.

What was the big hurry?

Lumpy breakfast mush—even soaked in molasses—was nothing to get in a hurry about.

Jem dumped the sand, gravel, and water from his gold pan. He rubbed the mud off his pants.

Then he ran back to the tent on his family's gold claim.

"The creek is full, Mama," Jem said, out of breath. "I have to eat fast and get back to—"

He stopped short.

His little sister, Ellie, sat on the split-log
bench at the outdoor table.

She was dressed in her best dress—the
one with the colored apron that she always
wore to Sunday school.

Only, today was not Sunday.

"Sit down and eat your breakfast," Mama said.

She plunked a bowl of steaming hot cereal down at Jem's place.

Jem sat. He and Ellie looked at each other.

"Why are you dressed up for Sunday school?" he asked.

For once, chatterbox Ellie didn't answer.

Instead, she spooned another bite of mush into her mouth and didn't say a word.

But her hand was shaking. She looked scared.

"For goodness' sake, Jem." Mama put her hands on her hips. "Today must have flown right out of your head."

Jem's eyebrows shot up. "What do you mean, Mama?"

"No gold panning today. You need to eat quick and change into clean clothes for school."

School! Jem groaned, but only to himself.

Mama was right. The first day of school had flown out of Jem's head as soon as he saw Cripple Creek.

No wonder Ellie was dressed up. But why did she look scared?

Jem nudged her. "You told me last spring you wished you could go to school."

Ellie shrugged.

"Now your wish is coming true." Jem swallowed his lumpy mush.

"I changed my mind," Ellie whispered. "I want to stay home and play with Nugget."

The golden dog lifted his head. *Woof!*

His tail thumped the ground.

For once, no dust puffed up. The dirt was too wet.

Jem wanted to stay home and play with Nugget too.

He wanted to pan gold in the swollen creek. He wanted to help Pa and their friend Strike-it-rich Sam wash gold in the rocker box.

"I bet the storm washed more gold down the creek," Jem said. "Can't I stay home and pan? Just for today?"

"Me too, Mama." Ellie raised her voice. "Just one more day?"

Mama shook her head. "I won't hear of you children missing even one day of school."

Jem didn't say anything out loud, but he was thinking a lot.

Learning the three Rs—reading, writing, and 'rithmetic—was important to Mama and Pa.

Very important.

Mama had more to say. "You children should be grateful. Goldtown has a good school. Miss Cheney is a fine teacher."

She sighed. "The teacher in Bootjack moved away, so now they have no school."

Mama made it sound like not having a school was the worst thing that could happen in a mining town.

Jem thought it would be the *best* thing that could happen. He secretly wished he lived in Bootjack.

Lucky ducks! The kids in Bootjack could run and play all day long.

They could pan for gold. They could explore old coyote holes.

They could—

Mama clapped her hands. "Enough daydreaming. You can't be late on the first day of school."

Jem washed down the last of his mush with four big gulps of water.

Mama shooed him into the tent to change. "Make sure you comb your hair," she called.

Jem changed his clothes, scrubbed his face in a bucket of cold water, and ran a comb through his dark hair.

When he returned, Mama handed him the tin lunch pail. "Look after your sister, Jeremiah. It's her first day of school."

"Yes, ma'am."

"And come straight home after school."

Jem nodded and started walking toward town.

Ellie dragged her feet behind him.

Woof! Nugget leaped up.

Mama caught the dog just in time. "You're staying home."

"Sorry, Nugget," Jem called over his shoulder.

Nugget whimpered and flopped to the ground beside Mama.

Halfway to school, Ellie grabbed Jem's hand.

He tried to peel away her fingers, but she wouldn't let go.

"You can't hold my hand all the way to school," Jem hissed. "What will the other kids say?"

Ellie held on tighter.

Jem rolled his eyes.

This was going to be his worst first day of school ever.

CHAPTER 2

First Day of School

Jem and Ellie walked into Goldtown half an hour later.

Big canvas tents spread out everywhere. Here and there, new wooden buildings poked up above the tents.

The town was still rebuilding after burning down last winter.

"Why are you so scared?" Jem asked. His hand felt crushed by Ellie's grip.

"I'm not scared." Ellie's face turned red. "Don't say that."

"Then let go of my hand."

Ellie let go. Her feet moved slower and slower.

Soon, she was far behind.

17

Jem turned around. "Hurry up, slowpoke. The teacher will punish us if we're late."

Miss Cheney was good at finding a corner for Jem to stand in.

Ellie scuffed the dirt and caught up. Mud stuck to her high-topped shoes.

"If you're not scared, then what's the matter?" Jem asked.

Ellie took a big breath and let it out. "Look." She spread her arms wide.

Jem looked. Then he shrugged. "At what?"

"My dress. It's—" A sob caught in her throat.

Jem took a closer look.

Ellie's once-white Sunday school dress had turned a dirty gray. The sleeves were too short.

Worse, Mama had sewed a patch on Ellie's apron. She had sewed a patch on her dress too.

Jem let out a big breath. "Who cares?" He started walking. "Wait till you see what the other kids wear to school."

"What?" Ellie asked.

"Patched overalls. Clothes that are too big. Or too small." Jem shrugged. "Scruffy stuff."

"Really?" Ellie ran to catch up. "No foolin'?"

"No fooling." Then he laughed. "Except rich Will, of course. He always dresses fancy."

Just then, the school bell rang. *Clang, clang, clang!*

Ellie's worried face turned smiley. She darted ahead.

"Come on, slowpoke," she hollered. "What are you waiting for?"

Jem rolled his eyes. One minute, Ellie looked ready to cry. Then quick as a passing rainstorm, her tears dried up.

Little sisters were so silly.

Jem climbed the five short steps and clomped into the classroom. He looked around.

Ellie was already inside. She had picked out a seat way up front and was sitting as still as a stone.

Like a wild bunny sniffing the air for danger, Jem thought.

Only, there wasn't any danger in this stuffy ol' classroom.

Jem sat down at his desk and grinned. "Hey, Perry! You came back to school."

His seatmate wrinkled his nose. "Ma always makes me go the first week."

Perry was right about that. In no time at all, he'd be back in Two-bit Gulch, panning gold with his pa.

Lucky duck!

Just then, Will Sterling slid into his seat across the aisle from Jem. He wore his fancy dark-blue jacket and snow-white Sunday shirt.

Like always.

"Howdy, Jem."

Jem's eyebrows shot up in surprise. He didn't know what to say.

Why was Will talking so friendly? That mean rich boy was *never* friendly.

At least not to Jem and Ellie.

Jem and Perry looked at each other. Will was not friendly to Perry, either.

Perry shrugged and turned his head away.

Jem wanted to turn his head away too. He wanted to tell Will to leave him alone.

But he didn't.

Every time Jem wanted to say something mean to Will, a Bible verse popped into his head.

This time it was a verse about being friendly. *A man that hath friends must show himself friendly.*

"Howdy, Will," Jem said at last.

That was as friendly as he could be this morning.

Will pointed to the front row. "Did you see my little sister?"

Jem shook his head. He didn't pay attention to other boys' sisters.

Especially not to Will's sister, Maybelle.

He looked to where Will was pointing.

Maybelle was a prissy thing. Today she wore a frilly dress with bows and lace.

She was sitting next to Ellie.

Poor Ellie, Jem thought. Her dark-red braids looked scraggly next to Maybelle's long curls and fancy hat.

"I want you to tell Ellie to play with Maybelle today," Will said.

"Huh?" Jem stared at Will. "Why?"

"Because it's Maybelle's first day of school."

"So what?"

"She's scared," Will said. "And I don't want her tagging around after me. If Ellie plays with her, then I won't have to."

No wonder Will had been friendly to Jem. He wanted something.

He wanted Jem to make Ellie play with prissy Maybelle.

Jem laughed on the inside. Will didn't know Ellie very well.

Nothing Jem could say would make Ellie play with Maybelle. Not if she didn't want to.

"Please, Jem," Will pleaded. "Will you do it?"

Jem just looked at him.

Will leaned across the aisle. "I saw something this morning on the way to school. Something you might want to see."

"What is it?" Jem asked.

Perry poked his head around Jem. "What did you see, Will?"

"I'm not telling." Will's face turned sneaky. "I'll show you after school, but only if Jem gets Ellie to play with Maybelle."

Jem wanted to say no, but he didn't. He was too curious.

What had Will seen?

"Oh, all right," he told Will. "But it better be worth it."

Will laughed. "It will be. I promise."

CHAPTER 3

Something to See

All morning, Jem thought about what he would say to Ellie.

Ideas spun around in his head. *Please play with Maybelle.*

Or . . . *She looks lonely. Why don't you play with her?*

Or . . . *If you don't play with her, nobody will.*

Or worse . . . *I'll pay you a pinch of gold dust if you play with Maybelle.*

Jem made a face. None of his ideas would work.

Ellie was too smart. She would know right away that Jem was trying to talk her into something.

He slumped.

Then Jem got an idea. An *excellent* idea.

He would tell Ellie the truth.

She was as curious as Jem. She would want to see what Will was going to show him.

And she would play with Maybelle to see it.

Jem cheered up after that.

He stood at the blackboard and worked his 'rithmetic problems with his whole heart. He didn't miss even one.

Miss Cheney said "good job" and let Jem erase the board.

When recess came, Jem waited for Ellie.

He waited while the big boys and the little boys raced out of the classroom.

He waited while the big girls hurried after the boys.

Where were Ellie and Maybelle? They were the only first graders in the school.

Then Jem saw them.

The two little girls were holding hands. They giggled and skipped up the aisle together.

Ellie didn't even look at Jem.

Jem's heart gave a happy leap. He didn't have to talk Ellie into anything.

He didn't have to tell Will anything either.
Jem grinned and ran outside to play.

· ★ ★ ★ ·

Will was all smiles after school.
"I don't know how you did it," he said.
"Ellie played with Maybelle every recess."
Jem wanted to keep quiet. He wanted
Will to think he'd talked Ellie into playing
with Maybelle.
But he had to tell Will the truth.

26

Even if it meant that mean rich boy would change his mind about showing Jem something.

"I didn't have to tell her," he said. "They just ran outside together."

Will's eyebrows went up, like he didn't believe Jem.

Then he smiled wider and tugged on Jem's sleeve. "Come on. I'll show you what I saw."

He took the school steps in one big leap. "Hurry!"

Jem jumped off the porch and ran after Will.

His heart thumped. What would Will show him?

Halfway through town, Will pointed to a tall wooden pole. "Look!"

Jem's feet came to a stop. "A telegraph pole. So what?"

There were lots of telegraph poles in Goldtown. Wires ran from one pole to the next, up and down Main Street.

Messages came through the wires. Some came from faraway San Francisco. Or Sacramento.

Will let out a big breath. "Not the pole, Jem. See what's *on* it."

A sheet of heavy paper was nailed to the pole.

Just then, Perry and Cole ran up.

Perry whooped. "A Wanted poster!"

The two boys ran past Jem and Will.

Jem scowled. *This* was the secret something Will wanted to show him?

A Wanted poster?

Jem had seen Wanted posters before. They were nothing new. Or special.

Or anything Jem wanted to see.

Will followed Perry and Cole to the telegraph pole.

Jem sighed. He might as well see which miner had turned into an outlaw this week.

He wondered what the miner had done to get his face on a Wanted poster.

Had he stolen another miner's gold claim? Had he run off with someone's prospecting tools?

Maybe—Jem shivered—maybe this new outlaw had killed another miner.

Anything could happen in a gold-mining camp.

By the time Jem had joined the others at the pole, a little bug of excitement was pinching his thoughts.

Maybe a new outlaw would be something to see, after all.

Jem pushed his way between Cole and Will. He looked up at the large piece of paper.

It was not a Wanted poster.

The drawing didn't show a scruffy miner with a slouch hat, a beard, and mean eyes. The words did not talk about any outlaws.

It was a Reward poster. The drawing showed a dog.

The nice-looking dog had floppy ears, a friendly face, and a long, fluffy tail.

There were words above and below the drawing.

Will read the words out loud. "Reward. Two thousand dollars."

Cole whistled. "That's sure a lot of money!"

Will nodded and kept reading. "Lost Dog. Golden retriever Golden Jubilee. Last seen March tenth near Mariposa."

Jem stared at the poster.

"Notify Mister Carson MacRae in Sacramento," Will finished.

He turned around and looked at Jem. "That drawing looks kind of like your mutt, don't you think?"

Jem didn't answer. He couldn't. His throat felt as dry as dust.

The drawing on the Reward poster did not look "kind of like" his dog, Nugget.

It looked *exactly* like him.

CHAPTER 4

The Reward Poster

Jem stared at the poster for a whole minute.

He didn't realize he was holding his breath until it came out all at once. "No!"

It couldn't be true.

"Nugget is *my* dog," Jem said.

Strike-it-rich Sam had found the half-grown pup on a prospecting trip. The poor dog had been half starved.

Strike had brought Nugget home and given him to Jem and Ellie.

Now, Gold Nugget was as much a part of the Coulter family as Strike was.

Jem's fingers curled into tight fists. "The dog on this poster must be a different one."

"A man was nailing the poster to the pole

when I walked by this morning," Will said. "I told you this was something you might want to see."

Will was right about that. For sure Jem wanted to see this.

But what could he do about it?

Slowly, his fingers began to relax.

Will was still talking. "I don't see how that mutt of yours could be worth two thousand dollars."

"I wish he was *my* dog," Perry said. "I'd send a telegram to that Mr. MacRae fellow as quick as I could."

"Yeah," Cole agreed. "Do you know how long it takes to pan two thousand dollars' worth of gold?"

Jem knew. It made his head spin to think about so much money.

"It's not the same dog," he said.

Please, God, don't let it be my dog, he prayed from his heart.

Will reached up high. He put a finger on the date. March 10.

"Didn't Strike find your mutt last spring?"

Jem didn't answer.

REWARD
$2000

LOST DOG
Golden retriever Golden Jubilee
Last seen MARCH 10th near Mariposa
Notify Mr. Carson MacRae in
SACRAMENTO

"I bet you a dime it's the same dog," Will said.

"No, it's not!"

Will crossed his arms. "I'm going to ask my father to send a telegram to Mr. MacRae."

The other boys gasped.

"You better not!" Jem yelled.

Leave it to Will to do such a mean thing. Will didn't like Nugget. Not one bit.

Not since Nugget had growled at Will on pie-delivery day last spring.

That mean rich boy couldn't pick on Jem and Ellie anymore. Nugget always scared him away.

Will would be glad if Nugget left Goldtown.

"When Father sends the telegram, Mr. MacRae will come to Goldtown," Will was saying. "And I'll get the reward."

He turned and ran off. "All two thousand dollars!" he shouted.

Jem felt sick. *No, no, no!*

His fingers itched to tear that awful poster off the pole. He wanted to rip it into a million pieces.

But he didn't.

Ripping up Mr. MacRae's Reward poster was almost like stealing.

Jem looked at his friends.

"I wouldn't really telegraph Mr. MacRae," Perry said. "I was just talking."

"I know." Jem sighed. "Me neither. Not even if the reward for Nugget was a million dollars."

Jem's friends gave the poster one last glance.

Then Perry left. It was a long walk out to Two-bit Gulch, where he lived.

"Bye, Jem," Cole said and took off for home.

Jem stood alone and stared at the poster. The more he studied the drawing, the more it looked like Nugget.

His Nugget.

CHAPTER 5
Trouble

Jem was still staring at the poster when Ellie tugged on his sleeve.

"What are you doing?" she asked. "I've been looking for you all over the place."

Jem caught his breath. Mama's words from this morning stung him.

"Look after your sister."

He had forgotten all about Ellie.

But Ellie didn't look scared. She didn't look lost. She looked full of questions.

Like always.

"Why are you staring at that paper?" She shaded her eyes against the afternoon sun. "Is that a picture of a dog?"

Jem's heart was too full of misery to answer.

Ellie yanked his sleeve harder. "Jem! What's—"

"Nothing," he snapped. "Let's go home."

He shook free of Ellie's clutching fingers and stomped off down the street.

Ellie didn't follow him. She stayed right where she was.

Jem glanced over his shoulder.

His little sister stood on tiptoes, leaning against the pole. She tipped her head way back.

"Come on!" Jem shouted.

Ellie looked at Jem. She looked at the poster. Then she ran to catch up.

Right away she started asking questions.

"Is that Nugget? Why is our dog on that poster? Who put it up? What does it say?"

Jem was glad Ellie couldn't read the words herself.

He wished *he* couldn't read the words.

"Tell me what it says," Ellie begged. "Please!"

"Be patient with your sister."

For once, Jem didn't listen to Mama's words. "No!"

Ellie's eyes grew round. She bit her lip and sniffed. But she didn't cry.

Not yet, anyway.

"Never mind what the poster says," Jem said. "Let's go home."

Mama's other words sneaked into his head. *"Come straight home after school."*

Jem's belly did a flip. He and Ellie had not gone straight home after school.

I had to see what Will wanted to show me, he thought. *I just had to.*

Part of Jem was glad he had seen the poster.

The other part was not glad. He and Ellie should not have stayed in town so long.

"Hurry up." He grabbed Ellie's hand and pulled her along. "We better get home before Pa comes looking for us."

Too late.

Woof! A happy bark filled the air. An instant later, Nugget circled Jem and Ellie.

His tail swished back and forth. His tongue licked Jem's hand.

The golden dog wriggled with joy.

Jem dropped to the ground. He threw his arms around Nugget's neck and squeezed him tight.

"I love you, Nugget," he whispered.

Jem didn't want to let Nugget go. Not ever.

"Jeremiah."

Jem looked up. Pa's brown eyes were usually warm and laughing.

Not today.

Today, Pa's eyes had a scolding look in them.

Uh-oh. Jem was in big trouble. "Howdy, P-pa," he stammered.

He kept one hand on Nugget's shiny, golden head and stood up.

Pa looked at Jem and Ellie. He didn't say anything for a whole minute.

Then he let out a long sigh. "You worried your mother today, Jeremiah. She thought you were old enough to take your sister to school and bring her home safely."

"I *am* old enough," Jem said. "We deliver pies in town all by ourselves. I watch out for Ellie every Saturday."

"That's true," Pa said. "But you always come straight home. Why not today?"

Jem's fingers curled around Nugget's soft fur. He did not have a good answer for Pa.

"I know why Jem didn't go home." Ellie leaped away from Nugget. "I'll show you."

She grabbed Pa's hand and started pulling him down the street. She headed straight for the telegraph pole.

A minute later, Pa was reading the poster.

"Read it to me, Pa!" Ellie begged.

Jem held his breath. This was not a good idea. Ellie might start crying.

Pa read the writing. The words sounded even worse this time.

"Will's father is going to send a telegram to Mr. MacRae," Jem told Pa.

"Hmm," Pa said.

Jem swallowed. "It's not Nugget, is it?"

"Please say it's not," Ellie said, blinking back tears.

Pa didn't answer. Instead, he reached up and carefully took down the poster.

Jem's eyes opened wide. Was Pa stealing Mr. MacRae's Reward poster?

"Can you do that?" he asked.

"I don't see why not. I'd like to have it when Mr. MacRae comes to town."

"What if he comes looking for his poster?" Jem asked.

Pa rolled up the poster and tucked it inside his vest. "I think Mr. MacRae will be more interested in looking for his dog."

Pa was right about that.

A big lump got stuck in Jem's throat. His next words came out in a whisper.

"What if Nugget really is Mr. MacRae's Golden Jubilee?"

Pa smiled. "Let's not worry about that right now."

"But, Pa!" Jem choked back a sob. "What will we do?"

Ellie started crying. "I don't want Nugget to go away!"

Pa swung Ellie up in his arms. "Take it easy, Ellianna."

His large, strong fingers curled around Jem's hand. "It's not time to worry, Son. It's time to pray."

Then Pa closed his eyes and prayed. Right in the middle of Main Street.

CHAPTER 6

Unwelcome Visitor

"Hullo! May I come up?"

The stranger's polite words echoed across Cripple Creek. He talked funny.

But not as funny as he looked.

The man was tall and skinny. His top hat made him look even taller. He was dressed all in black. A black umbrella was hooked over his arm.

An umbrella?

Jem looked up at the sky. No rain in sight.

He dumped out his gold pan and hurried back to the tent.

Pa was already there. So were Mama, Ellie, and Strike-it-rich Sam.

Something else was there too.

A bright golden dog lay at the man's feet.

Jem caught his breath. It was a beautiful dog.

The stranger shook Pa's hand. "Allow me to introduce myself. Carson MacRae of Cannich, Scotland."

He petted the dog. "This is Lady Promise."

"I'm Matt Coulter."

"Delighted to meet you," Mr. MacRae said.

Pa told Mr. MacRae Mama's name. He told him Jem's and Ellie's and Strike's names.

But Pa did not say he was delighted to meet him.

Nobody was delighted to meet Mr. Carson MacRae. Or his fancy dog.

Especially not Jem.

Jem's whole week had been one big misery.

Will had shown him a telegram from Mr. MacRae. *"Mr. Carson MacRae is coming to Goldtown."*

Will's message had buzzed around inside Jem's head like a swarm of angry bees.

"Mr. Carson MacRae is coming to Goldtown."

Now the stranger was here.

"Mr. Sterling kindly pointed the way out to your claim." He glanced around. "'Tis a real California gold claim, is it not?"

"Yes," Pa said.

Mr. MacRae shrugged. "'Tisn't much to look at."

What a rude man! Jem thought.

Pa was a gentleman. His eyes flashed, but all he said was, "We make do."

"Aye." Mr. MacRae cleared his throat. "I'm sure you do."

He tapped the pointed end of his umbrella on the ground. "You know why I'm here?"

"Yes." Pa found the poster and unrolled it.

"That's Golden Jubilee," Mr. MacRae said with a pleased smile.

He shaded his eyes and glanced around the camp. "Where is the poor laddie?"

"That's a good question," Mama said. She eyed Jem. "Go get him."

Strike laughed. "He's probably off chasing turkeys."

Jem didn't laugh. He didn't even smile.

He dragged his feet to the creek while the grown-ups sat down to talk.

"Nugget!" he called.

Jem hoped Nugget wouldn't come. His dog didn't like strangers.

Maybe Nugget would stay far away until Mr. MacRae got tired of waiting.

Woof! Nugget bounded out from between two pine trees.

He splashed through the muddy creek and nosed Jem's hand. His tail wagged back and forth.

Jem sighed. Nugget hadn't stayed away.

"I want you to growl at the stranger," he told him. "Maybe even bite him."

He chewed on his lip. What would Pa and Mama say about Jem's unkind words?

"I don't care," he whispered. His heart hurt too much.

Jem walked slower than a turtle back to camp. He kicked rocks. He found a stick and threw it.

Nugget leaped and caught the stick in the air.

Tears burned Jem's eyes. *No crying!*

Mr. MacRae was still looking at the

Reward poster when Jem brought Nugget
back.

The dog licked Ellie's hand. He greeted
Pa and Ma and Strike.

Then he saw the man and the strange dog.

Nugget froze. His nose quivered. His tail
swished two times.

Then he trotted up to Mr. MacRae and
laid his golden head on his lap.

Mr. MacRae dropped the poster and
rubbed Nugget's head. "Och, Jube, how
much you've grown!"

The next instant, Nugget and the other dog greeted each other.

Tails wagged. Their noses touched.

With a happy yip, the two dogs took off. They ran and leaped and tumbled over each other.

Mr. MacRae smiled. "Such a grand sight!"

Jem slumped. Mr. MacRae was not a stranger. Neither was his dog.

Nugget knew them both.

Ellie burst into tears. She jumped up and ran inside the tent.

Jem wanted to run and hide too, but he didn't.

Mr. MacRae was telling his story.

"Golden Jubilee and Lady Promise are the first of a new breed of dogs," the man said. "Golden retrievers."

He's got the golden part right, Jem thought.

"I brought my pair on a tour to your West Coast. Dog shows are just getting started in Great Britain."

Jem's eyebrows went up. People went to shows? To look at dogs?

That sounded silly.

"An accident near Mariposa overturned our stagecoach," Mr. MacRae said.

Mama gasped. "How awful!"

"Aye, it was," Mr. MacRae agreed. "We passengers and the driver were knocked out cold. Lady Promise was tangled up in her leash, but Jubilee . . ."

He shook his head. "Poor Jube was only a half-grown pup. When I came to, he was gone."

Happy barking made Jem turn his head.

Nugget and Lady Promise were chasing each other around coyote holes. They crossed the creek.

Then they darted into the woods.

Jem couldn't hold back his tears. He jumped up and ran inside the tent.

Just like Ellie.

CHAPTER 7

Jem's Not-So-Great Idea

Mr. MacRae stayed for a long time.

Mama served him coffee. She gave him a slice of blueberry pie.

But Mama didn't bake pies to sell to the miners. Not today. It wouldn't be polite to work when a guest was visiting.

Especially if the guest looked like a rich man from the other side of the world.

"I've been looking for Jubilee for six months," Mr. MacRae was saying.

Strike squinted at him. "Are you *sure* it's the same dog?"

Hurrah for Strike! Jem thought.

But he knew better.

"Aye. Quite sure." Mr. MacRae pointed under a tall pine tree. "Look at them. True friends. Someday they will have lovely pups."

The dogs lay asleep in the shade. They looked worn out and perfectly content.

A sharp pain stabbed Jem's belly.

Mr. MacRae would take Nugget with him back to Scotland.

"Please don't take Nugget." The words spilled out before Jem could stop himself.

"I'm sorry, laddie," Mr. MacRae said. "Jubilee is a valuable dog."

Pa crossed his arms. "If Strike hadn't found him, your valuable dog would be lost for good."

"'Tis true," Mr. MacRae agreed. "And I thank you kindly for saving him. Your family has earned the reward money."

"I don't want two thousand dollars!" Jem shouted.

"Jeremiah," Mama warned.

"Me neither!" Ellie shrieked. "I want Nugget!"

She ran to the pine tree and fell on top of Nugget.

He woke up and wagged his tail.

"We don't want your reward money, Mr. MacRae," Pa said softly. "We want to keep our dog."

"He's *my* dog." Mr. MacRae stood up. "I apologize. I believe I've overstayed my visit."

He picked up his umbrella. "Good day."

Jem caught his breath. "Pa!"

"I'm sorry, Jem." Pa sounded sad.

Mr. MacRae whistled. Lady Promise obeyed instantly.

Nugget wriggled out from under Ellie and followed Lady Promise.

Soon, both dogs sat in front of Mr. MacRae.

The Scotsman looked at the dogs. He looked at Jem and Ellie.

Then he sighed. "I leave tomorrow morning, Mr. Coulter. Perhaps your family would like until then to say good-bye?"

Pa nodded.

"Bring Jubilee to town at eight o'clock," Mr. MacRae said. "I'll have your reward money."

He hooked his umbrella over his wrist. "Stay," he told Nugget.

Then he and Lady Promise walked away.

Nugget whined, like he was puzzled. He sat still until Mr. MacRae and the other dog were gone.

Then Nugget nudged Jem's hand. *Woof! Let's go play*, he seemed to be saying.

Jem played with Nugget the rest of the afternoon.

He and Ellie threw sticks. They splashed in Bullfrog Pond. They played tug-of-war with an old rag.

Grrr! Nugget's teeth sank into the rag. He shook his head back and forth.

By evening, Nugget was worn out. He plopped under the pine tree and took a nap.

Jem sat next to his dog and stroked his head.

Ellie sat down too. "What are we going to do?" she asked in a tiny voice.

"Shh. I'm thinking."

"What about?" Ellie asked.

"About what we can do to keep Nugget."

Ellie's eyes grew big. "What are you—"

"Roasted rattlesnakes, Ellie! Stop asking questions."

Ellie crossed her arms and slouched. But she kept quiet.

Jem thought hard. How *could* he keep Nugget in Goldtown?

He closed his eyes and thought some more.

Then Jem got an idea. A *great* idea.

His eyes popped open. He smiled.

What if Nugget got lost again? A lost dog would be hard to find.

Would Mr. MacRae stay and look for Nugget? Maybe he would give up and go back to Scotland.

Jem cupped his chin in his hands.

Ellie looked at him. "Did you think of something?"

"Yes," Jem said. "But I can't tell you."

"Why not?"

Jem stood up and brushed the pine needles off his pants. "Because I have to do this by myself."

He could not take Ellie with him.

It was one kind of trouble to lose a dog in the woods.

It was trouble with a capital T to lose a sister in the woods.

"You *better* tell me," Ellie said. She wrinkled her eyebrows. "Or I'll—"

Jem grabbed her shoulders. "Do you want to keep Nugget?"

Ellie bit her lip and nodded. A tear dripped down her cheek.

"Then let me do this."

Two more tears dripped from Ellie's eyes. She sniffed. "All right."

"Good." Jem let out a big breath.

"Will you get in trouble?" Ellie whispered.

The worst ever, Jem thought. But he didn't say those words out loud.

"Probably," he said instead. "But keeping Nugget is worth it."

His heart pounded like drumbeats. *Thump, thump, thump.* It would not stop pounding.

Shivers went up and down Jem's arms at what he was about to do.

Jem's great idea suddenly felt like a not-so-great idea.

I have to do this, he told himself.

If he didn't, Jem would lose Nugget forever.

CHAPTER 8

A Night in the Woods

Jem lay awake for a long time that night.

He listened to Mama, Pa, and Strike talk around the fire. They talked and talked and talked.

Jem let out an impatient breath. When would they go to bed?

Finally, when it was as dark as the inside of a coyote hole, Pa and Mama told Strike good night.

Jem pulled the blanket around his shoulders. Maybe Mama wouldn't notice he was wearing his day clothes.

He yawned and waited some more. Did grown-ups *ever* go to bed?

Finally, Pa's quiet snores told Jem that his whole family was asleep.

At last!

Jem pushed the covers away and slipped off his cot. Next, he picked up his boots.

Then he tiptoed outside.

The moon was not full tonight. A pale half moon was rising over the mountains.

It was very late. Probably close to midnight.

"I guess half a moon is better than no moon," Jem whispered, pulling on his boots.

Nugget crawled out from under the table. He yawned. His tail wagged.

"Shh." Jem found a long rope and tied a loop around his dog's neck.

"Come on, Nugget. We have a long way to go."

Jem led Nugget upstream. He didn't know exactly where he was going.

Only that he was taking Nugget far away into the woods.

He shivered. The pine trees rose tall and dark. The woods went on and on.

There wasn't even a trail.

The moon barely shone between the tree

branches. It would be easy to lose Nugget in these woods.

"I hope I don't get lost too," Jem whispered.

He listened for Cripple Creek. It trickled not too far away.

Good. As long as Jem could find the creek, he wouldn't get lost.

After what seemed like hours, Jem stopped next to a small pine tree. He tied one end of the rope around the trunk.

"I'm sorry, Nugget," Jem said. "You have to stay here until Mr. MacRae goes home."

Woof! Nugget licked Jem's cheek.

"I have to go home, but I'll bring you food and water tomorrow."

Nugget whined.

Jem sat down and put his arms around Nugget's neck. "Please stay here. I have to make it look like you're lost."

Nugget didn't want to stay in the dark. He tugged at the leash. He chewed the rope.

A little bee of worry stung Jem's thoughts. Hiding Nugget in the woods was almost like stealing.

Or was it?

Pa's quiet words to Mr. MacRae made Jem feel better. *"We want to keep our dog."*

Our dog, Jem thought. *Not Mr. MacRae's.*

Even Pa talked like Nugget was their own dog.

Jem ruffled Nugget's fur and stood up. "I have to go home. You lie down. Go to sleep."

Nugget cocked his head at Jem. He barked.

"Shh!" Jem put a finger to his lips. "No barking."

A dog's bark could be heard for a long way. Maybe even all the way back to the Coulter gold claim.

If Pa heard that barking, Nugget would not stay lost for long.

Jem sat on the ground again and pulled Nugget down next to him. "I'll stay here until you get used to this spot."

Nugget got used to it right away. He rested his head on his paws and closed his eyes.

Yawning, Jem snuggled next to Nugget. "I can only stay for a minute."

His eyes closed, and Jem fell asleep.

Just like that.

· ★ ★ ★ ·

Jem woke up all at once. *Oh, no!*

He rubbed his eyes and looked around. The sun was just coming up.

The woods were alive with morning sounds. Songbirds chirped. Chipmunks chattered. Crows cawed.

Nugget was still sleeping.

As quietly as he could, Jem rose.

Nugget's head popped up. He looked at Jem, but he didn't bark.

"Good dog," Jem whispered. "Stay."

Nugget thumped his tail on the ground and buried his nose in his paws.

Jem grinned. Nugget was used to being tied up during the day.

Mama tied up Nugget every morning, so he wouldn't follow Jem and Ellie to school.

Jem tied up Nugget when he went to the pond to catch bullfrogs for the café.

The golden dog never barked then. He wouldn't bark now.

"Good dog," Jem said again. "I'll be back later."

He turned and darted through the woods.

He had to get home fast—before Mama and Pa saw that he was missing.

Jem ran and ran.

When he found the creek, he didn't stop. He splashed through the shallow water and kept running.

Jem followed Cripple Creek all the way

home. When he got to the tent, he stopped and listened.

Nobody was up yet.

Jem tiptoed inside, pulled off his boots, and crawled under his covers.

Wet socks and all.

He didn't go to sleep. He was too busy thinking.

Pa would have to tell Mr. MacRae that Nugget was lost.

When Pa goes to town, I'll take care of Nugget, Jem thought with a smile.

He would take him food and water every day. Nugget would stay lost until Mr. MacRae went back to Scotland.

Just then, a scary thought turned Jem's happy plans upside down.

How would he find Nugget?

Jem had not marked his path. He never looked back to see where he went into the woods.

I was in too big of a hurry to get home, he thought.

A big lump got stuck in his throat. He swallowed.

Nugget might really and truly be lost.

CHAPTER 9

Danger!

"Jem! Jem!" Ellie shook him. "Wake up."

Jem blinked. His eyes felt gritty.

Bright sunshine lit up the inside of the tent.

He groaned. "Go away."

Ellie shook him harder. "Pa can't find Nugget. He's called and called."

Jem's heart skipped. He threw off his covers and sat up.

Ellie's eyes opened wide. "Why did you wear your day clothes to bed?"

"That's a very good question."

Jem looked up. Pa was standing by the tent flap. His eyes looked full of worry.

Heat crept up Jem's neck and into his cheeks.

Mama came inside. She saw Jem's red face. "Oh, Jeremiah, what have you done?"

He didn't answer. His tongue was stuck.

"Answer your mother," Pa said. He meant business.

Jem's tongue got unstuck in a hurry. He told Pa and Mama the whole story.

Even the part about how Nugget might really be lost.

Tears spilled. Hot, frightened tears. "I'm sorry. I'm sorry."

Mama sat down on Jem's cot. She pulled him onto her lap and held him tight.

Pa didn't sit down. He pushed the tent flap away. "I'll go into town and try to explain this to Mr. MacRae."

He shook his head sadly. "There's a chance that Nugget might die out there, Son."

Jem sobbed louder. "I know."

It was not easy to find someone lost in the woods. Jem remembered how scared the grown-ups had been when Ellie got lost last spring.

Jem's not-so-great idea had turned into his worst idea ever!

When he stopped crying, Pa was gone.

Mama made Jem eat breakfast, even though he didn't want to. The lumpy mush almost came back up.

It seemed like hours before Pa came home.

Mr. MacRae was with him. So was his pretty golden dog, Lady Promise.

Jem wanted to run and hide. He didn't want to face the angry Scotsman.

But Jem got a big surprise.

Mr. MacRae didn't look angry. He smiled and sat down on a stump.

"Och, laddie," he told Jem. "Don't worry. Lady Promise will find Jubilee."

Jem's heart leaped.

"You're going with him, Jem," Pa said. "Bring Nugget back."

Jem jumped up to obey. "Yes, Pa."

"I want to go too," Ellie begged.

Pa shook his head. "This is between Jem, Nugget, and Mr. MacRae."

Lady Promise raced for the creek. Jem and Mr. MacRae set off after her.

Nobody said a word.

Jem was too ashamed to talk. Mr. MacRae was breathing too hard to talk.

Jem could run and think at the same time.

His heart hurt to lose Nugget.

But it was better to let Lady Promise find Nugget. It was better for Nugget to go to Scotland than to be tied up and lost in the woods.

Jem was learning his lesson the hard way.

Soon, barking and yipping told Jem that Nugget had been found.

He glanced back at Mr. MacRae. "Hurry!" Then he ran faster.

"Aye, laddie." The man panted. His steps slowed. "I'm coming."

Jem pushed through the brush and small pine trees. "Nugget!"

Nugget went wild with joy. He lurched against his rope leash. *Woof!*

Jem loosened the rope and lifted the loop over Nugget's head.

Lady Promise turned aside and nosed the ground. Then she poked her nose into some bushes.

Jem grinned. There were so many strange new scents for a dog to explore.

The golden retriever flushed out a squirrel. It scolded Lady Promise and ran up a tree.

Jem held Nugget tight. This might be the last time he would ever hug and pet his dog.

But Nugget wouldn't sit still. He wriggled from Jem's grip and joined Lady Promise.

"You better not chase turkeys today," Jem warned. "Mr. MacRae won't like it if—"

Bzzzz.

Jem froze. Nugget froze.

Lady Promise nosed deeper into the bushes.

The buzzing grew louder.

Nugget sprang to Lady Promise's side. He yipped a warning and nudged her away from the underbrush.

Then Nugget yelped and jumped back. Whining, he rubbed his face on the ground.

He shook his head, pawed his nose, and whined some more.

Jem's heart dropped to his belly. "No!"

Mr. MacRae pushed into the clearing. "What's going on?"

"Rattlesnake!" Jem leaped into Mr. MacRae. "Get back!"

The Scotsman stumbled and fell backward. Jem landed on Mr. MacRae's stomach. *Oof!*

Lady Promise circled Nugget, whining.

From a safe distance, Jem watched a big rattlesnake slither away.

Nugget lay on the ground, whimpering. His face was already swelling up.

Please, God! Jem prayed silently. *Don't let Nugget die!*

Mr. MacRae sat up. He brushed the dirt and pine needles from his pants. "What happened?" He sounded scared.

"Nugget saved Lady Promise from a rattlesnake," Jem said in a shaky voice. "But he got bit."

Mr. MacRae's face turned white. "What can we do?"

"Nothing," Jem said. "Please, sir. Carry him home."

Mr. MacRae gently lifted Nugget and started walking.

Jem followed, blinking back tears.

By the time they reached the Coulter claim, Nugget was limp. His face looked huge. It was all swelled up.

In a rush of words, Jem told Pa what had happened.

Pa took Nugget and settled him on a blanket. "Poor fellow."

"Jubilee saved Lady Promise," Mr. MacRae said in a shaky voice. "And your boy pushed me out of the way." He swallowed. "Will the dog live?"

"Only God knows the answer to that," Pa said quietly. "But it doesn't look good."

Jem ran and hid inside the tent.

CHAPTER 10

Gold Nugget Telegram

Mr. MacRae did not stay long.

"Good-bye, laddie." He gently stroked Nugget's fur. "I'll miss you."

Nugget lay still. His tail didn't thump. He didn't raise his head.

Jem and Ellie, red-faced from crying, watched the Scotsman and Lady Promise leave.

Even Mama had tears in her eyes.

She and Pa took care of Nugget the rest of the day. Strike took care of him all night.

For two days everybody watched over Nugget. Everybody prayed.

When the golden dog was still alive on the third day, Jem began to hope.

Every day after school that week, Jem sat next to Nugget. "You have to get well," he said. "You just have to."

Then Jem got a big surprise.

Nugget lifted his head. His tail thumped.

Jem sucked in a happy breath. "Pa!" he yelled. "Mama! Ellie! Strike!"

Ellie came running.

Mama left her washtub. Pa and Strike left their gold rocker.

They all squatted next to Nugget.

Strike whistled. "That is one tough dog."

"Will he be all right?" Ellie asked.

Pa nodded. "I think so."

Ellie squealed.

Jem grabbed her hands and spun her around. "Nugget's going to be fine!"

Pa and Mama smiled.

Every day, Nugget got better. The swelling in his face went down.

Jem saw two holes. The snake had bitten Nugget right above his eyes.

He turned to Pa in wonder. "How come Nugget didn't die, Pa?"

73

Pa pulled Jem onto one knee. He lifted Ellie onto his other knee.

"Nugget must have been bitten with only part of the snake's venom," he explained. "Just enough to make him really sick."

Jem wrinkled his eyebrows. "But not enough to kill him?"

Pa shook his head. "It might have been an old, lazy snake. Or maybe one that had just eaten."

"It did look fat," Jem remembered. "Maybe it had a mouse in its belly."

Ellie giggled.

"God was surely watching out for Nugget," Pa said.

Mama smiled. "All's well that ends well."

"Yep," Pa said. "There is nothing so bad that something good can't come out of it."

"How can anything good come out of Nugget getting bit by a nasty old snake?" Jem asked.

Pa chuckled. "Well, if Nugget had not been bitten, Mr. MacRae would have taken him back to Scotland."

Jem grinned. Pa was right about that!

"He only left Nugget behind because he thought he was going to die," Mama said.

Pa hugged Jem and Ellie. "Only somebody not used to the West would think that *all* rattlesnake bites mean death."

He winked at Jem. "Mr. MacRae didn't need to know *everything* about rattlesnakes."

"You're right, Pa," Ellie said, eyes wide.

Pa laughed. "Of course I'm right."

"Don't you remember the time Nine Toes got bit?" Strike asked. "Right on that big toe of his."

"I remember," Jem said.

"The miner was mighty sick, and he lost his big toe," Pa said. "But he lived."

"He learned to keep his boots on," Mama said. She looked long and hard at Jem and Ellie.

Jem knew what *that* look meant. *Keep your boots on even when it's hot.*

Maybe Mama knew what she was talking about. Jem did not want to lose *his* big toe to a rattlesnake.

Woof! Nugget rolled over and lifted his head. *Pay attention to me,* he seemed to be saying.

Jem and Ellie slipped from Pa's knees and ran over to their golden dog.

"You'll be back to normal in no time," Jem said. "Won't you, boy?"

Woof!

· ★ ★ ★ ·

"Jem Coulter! Come over here."

Jem frowned. What did Mr. Ames want?

Jem couldn't be late getting home from school today.

It was November, and the day before Thanksgiving. Jem wanted to go with Pa to shoot a wild turkey.

But he'd better find out what the shop-keeper wanted.

He grabbed Ellie's hand and hurried over to the new wooden store. "Yes, sir?"

Mr. Ames held out an envelope. "There's a telegram here with your name on it."

"*My* name?" Jem's eyebrows shot up. Telegrams cost a lot of money to send.

Who would send an eight-year-old boy a fancy telegram?

Mr. Ames handed Jem the envelope and went back inside.

"Well, read it," Ellie said.

Jem tore open the envelope and unfolded the piece of paper.

To: Jeremiah Coulter
Goldtown, Calif.

SORRY ABOUT GOLDEN JUBILEE.
LADY PROMISE HAD FIVE PUPS. YOUR
NUGGET LIVES ON.
CARSON MACRAE
CANNICH, SCOTLAND

Jem turned to Ellie. "Listen to this. Nugget's a father."

Ellie clapped her hands. "Yippee!"

She took off running for home.

"Hey!" Jem hollered. "This is my news!"

Ellie ran faster.

Jem raced after her. Then he slowed down. "Oh, all right."

He folded the telegram and slipped it into his pocket.

Jem suddenly didn't care if his chatterbox little sister told the whole world this good news!

A Peek into the Past: Rattlesnake Bites

A rattlesnake bite is dangerous. Even today, a person or an animal can get very sick from one.

In the past, snakebites were even more dangerous. Why? Because there were no emergency rooms or medicine to help heal a snakebite (this medicine is called antivenom).

The Yokut Indians of California made rattlesnake baskets. They put rattlesnakes in them. Every spring, parents paid the medicine man to dance around the basket to protect their children from getting bit.

Are all rattlesnake bites deadly? It depends on the snake.

The Northern Pacific rattlesnake is the snake Jem would have seen. Its bite is not as dangerous as the Mojave rattlesnake, which lives farther south. The Mojave rattlesnake is the deadliest rattlesnake in the United States.

Rattlesnakes don't always release their full load of venom. When this happens, the bite is less dangerous. The animal or person can live, even without treatment. This is the kind of bite Nugget received.

Also, rattlesnakes sometimes give "dry bites." This means they bite, but they don't inject any venom. The snake is giving you a big warning!

However, there is no way to tell how much venom a snake has injected, or if the snake has given you or your pet a dry bite. Always seek medical attention.

Stay away from rattlesnakes!

· ★ ★ ★ ·

Download free coloring pages and learning activities at GoldtownAdventures.com.